Written by Jessica Tilley

Illustrated by Natalie Thomson

For Cam

I pray you always speak from your heart and express yourself!

If you love someone, say it.

If you have to run, say it.

If your feelings hurt, say it

If you totally forgot, say it.

If you need a hug, say it.

If you totally messed up, say it.

When you want extra sweets, say it.

When your stomach aches from fear, say it.

When someone does something nice, say, "Thank you."

So you want to build a business, say it.

So your bike is on flat, say it.

So you really need a hat, say it.

Of all the things you do not choose
To say when needed you'll certainly lose.

The grandest opportunity
To share the you people need to see.

How many hills and valleys we create
In order to avoid the fate.

The fate of what is plain to see
The dreaded sheer transparency.

What awful woes might lie ahead
To say a thing, when instead.

The option is to close the door
That brings in light and life and more.

What can result from saying a thing? Does embarrassment or disappointment wait in the wings?

Could a positive response be what you find?
Could others be compassionate and kind?

Just put forth the effort. Don't keep your feelings at bay. What do you need to say today? Just exhale and say it, hooray!

About the Author

Jessica Tilley is an American children's book author. Her other published books are, "You Have To Be Smart If You're Going To Be Tall," and, "A Mother's Heart." In addition to working in education with children and youth she also enjoys spending time with her family as well as creating and selling hand-made jewelry. She hopes her books will influence children and their families to grow together by finding different ways to communicate and deal with everyday issues.